SPIKE in the KENNEL

Written and illustrated by
Paulette Bogan

G. P. Putnam's Sons   New York

Printed in Hong Kong by South China Printing Co. (1988) Ltd.
Designed by Gina DiMassi. Text set in Clichee Bold.
The art was done in watercolor.
Library of Congress Cataloging-in-Publication Data
Bogan, Paulette. Spike in the kennel / Paulette Bogan.
p. cm. Summary: On his first stay at a kennel, Spike is worried
about being left in a strange place, but when it is time to go home,
he wants to stay. [1. Dogs—Fiction. 2. Kennels—Fiction.]
I. Title. PZ7.B6339 Sp 2001 [E]—dc21 00-055357
ISBN 0-399-23594-9
1 3 5 7 9 10 8 6 4 2
First Impression

With love to
Rebecca for all her help
& Joshua, Andrew & David

It was Spike's first visit to the kennel.
"Don't worry," said Shannon. "You'll have fun."

But Spike was worried. The place smelled . . . doggy!
Shannon waved good-bye to him.

Then a new girl took Spike.

The girl led him down a long hall.
"AARRGGHH!" whined Spike.

The food smelled weird. "YEECH!" said Spike.

Outside there were dogs everywhere!

They were all playing together. Spike felt all alone.

The girl made Spike take a shower.

Spike slipped on the tiles and got soap in his eyes.

Then the girl blew hot air in his face.

"YEEOWZZA!" yelped Spike.

That night the cage was dark and scary.

Spike heard strange noises.

Poor Spike. He missed sleeping on Shannon's bed.
He missed Shannon!

"AARROOOO!" howled Spike.

Just as Spike began to fall asleep,
something scratched at his door.
A little dog was opening his cage.

All the dogs were sneaking out.

Outside everyone played Frisbee, even Spike.

"WOOF!" he barked.

Suddenly a light went on!

"What are you all doing out here?" shouted the girl.

They all lined up to go back inside.

But the girl was not angry. She gave them
each a treat and sent them back to bed.

The next morning Shannon was there!
"Are you ready to go home, Spike?"

SLURP! Spike gave Shannon a big kiss.

But Spike wasn't quite ready to go.